www.grandmasknittedkingdom.com

Inspired by my Nana Avril who loved to knit and Carol Mellard who still does.

For my little boy Jack

My Grandma lives in a knitted house.
It is actually made of wool.
She knitted for a hundred years
until her house was full.

Full of knitted curtains, flowers,
cushions, socks and hats.
Once a mouse came to her house
so she knitted five thousand traps.

Her bed is knitted.
Her clothes are knitted.

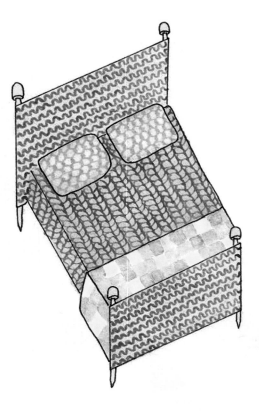

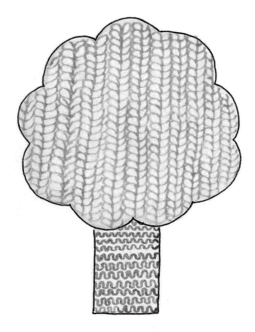

In her garden is a knitted tree.

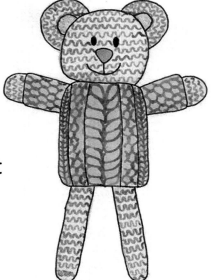

But my Grandma is at her happiest
when knitting toys for me.

I have a knitted ball,
a knitted teddy bear.
I have a knitted tea set,

and all the knitted clothes I could ever wear.

I used to wonder
about this hobby.
I admit,
I thought it strange

Why knit and knit
all day long?
Does she not
need a change?

I asked Grandma politely
'Would you like to do something new?'

She smiled at me
and excitedly said
'I think it's time you knew!'.

Her eyes lit up as she dropped her needles
and said 'Quick follow me'.
'Where are we going Grandma?' I asked.
She replied 'You'll see!'

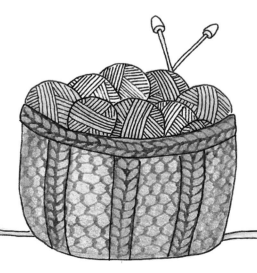

My Grandma ran to the kitchen,
then out of the back door.
I hadn't seen my Grandma run
for five years or maybe more.

She turned to me and said 'keep up!'
I ran as fast as I could
but she'd disappeared
and when I looked around
I was in a knitted wood!

With knitted birds, leaves and trees,
squirrels, owls and frogs.
In pure amazement I took a seat
on a knitted pile of logs.

The logs were soft
not hard as they would be
in places I usually go.

I looked to the sky
and to my surprise
from knitted clouds
fell snow!

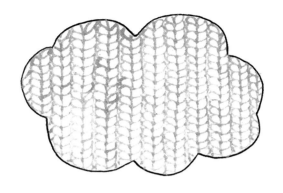

As the snow fell on my shoulders
I knew it should feel chilly,
but instead it was nice
and warm and soft.
I giggled, this all seemed silly.

I heard a giggle back
from far above my head.
Then came my Grandma's voice:
'Quick, up here' she said.

I looked and looked but could not find
my dear old knitting Grandma.
A knitted squirrel ran up a tree,
I whispered 'there you are'.

Safe in the knowledge I couldn't be hurt
from woolen sticks and stones
I climbed to my Grandma as fast as I could.
She was perched on a knitted throne.

My Grandma looked a vision
on the regal pearly chair,
wearing the most beautiful dress
and knitted flowers in her hair.

'So...what do you think?'
She beamed gleefully
'Of this world of my creation'.

Speechless I gazed out from the knitted tree
with pride and admiration.

'Grandma, where are we?' I asked finally.
'What is this beautiful place?'

My eyes more open than they'd ever been
and the biggest smile across my face

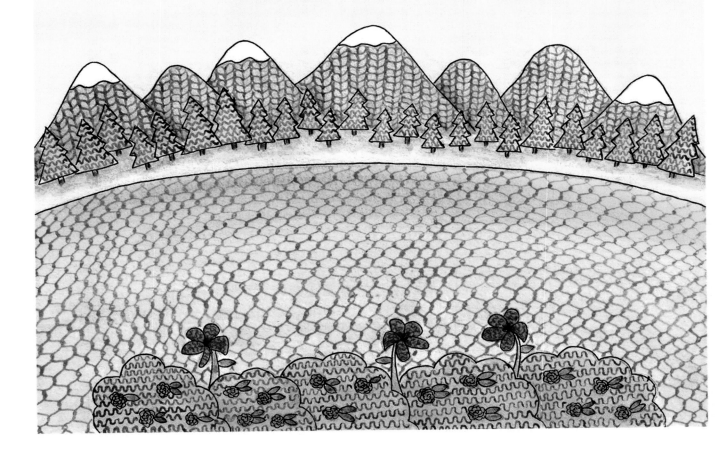

'You are in my kingdom sweetheart' she said
'All you see is mine!'
'I made the sky, the trees, the ground,
that leaf, that bird, that pine.

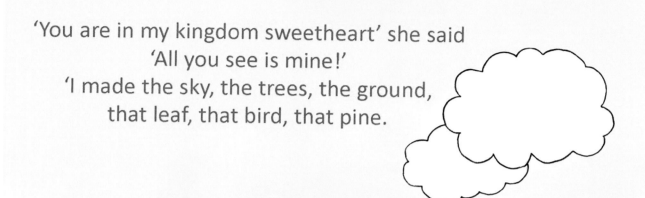

My own dear grandma sat and knitted
for hours and hours and hours
to make this tree, just for me,
then filled it with leaves and flowers.

When I first came to this place, you know,
there was only this one tree,
it is the only thing I did not make,
it was handed down to me.

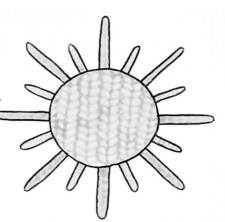

There came a day I questioned
why she loved to knit all day
and she brought me here as I have you
and this is what she had to say':

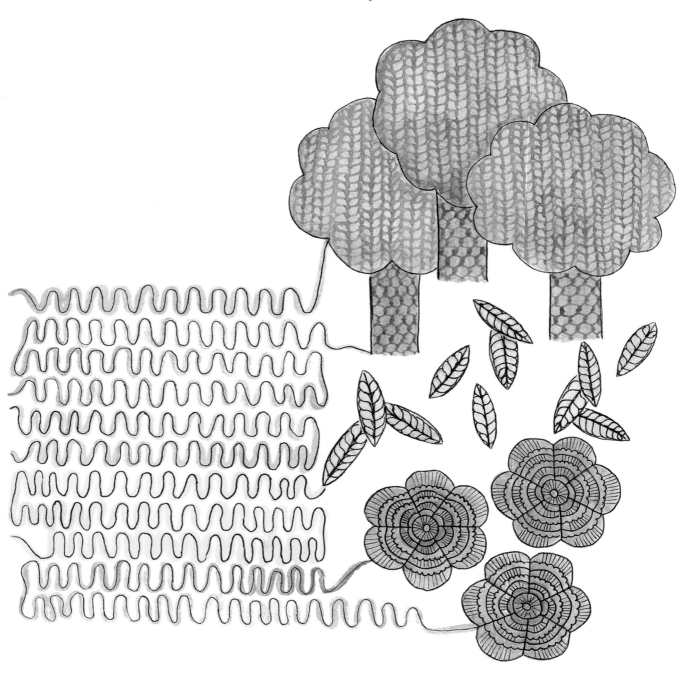

'When you were small
and the weather was cold
I knitted you a hat.

When you grew bigger,
you wanted a pet,
So I knitted you a cat.'

'My grandma had given me a place to play
where I could not be hurt.
No scratches or scrapes
or bruises or bumps,
no mud on my shirt.'

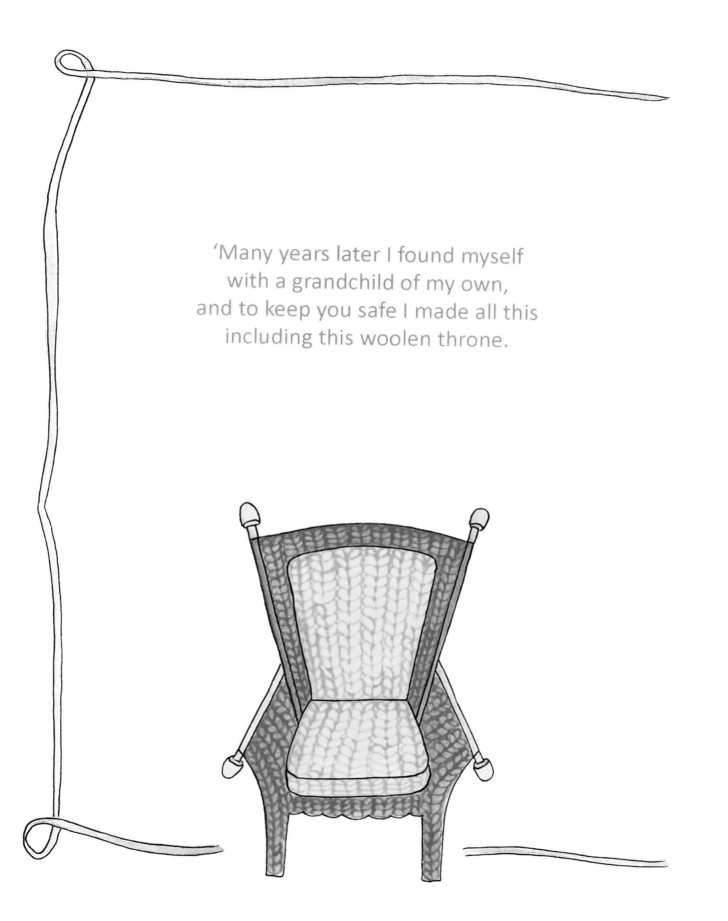

'Many years later I found myself
with a grandchild of my own,
and to keep you safe I made all this
including this woolen throne.

I always knew I'd bring you here
and I knew your face would glow.

With all the time I spend on this,
your curiosity would always grow.

There are enchanted lands
beyond those hills,
it is yours now to explore.

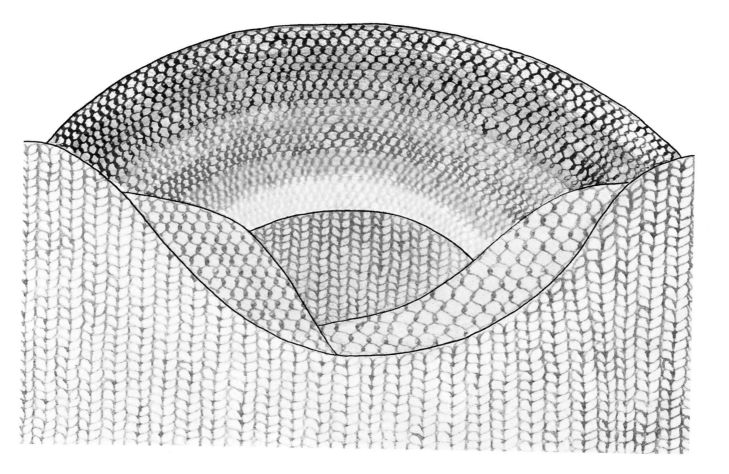

There are fairies, wood nymphs,
hummingbirds, caves, oceans
and so much more.

The time has come my darling
to pass this land to you.
Please take this map and compass
they will always guide you through.

'Before you begin your journey
there is one more thing to do.

A ceremony of passing this land
from your grandmother to you.'

All the creatures of the land crept out
from behind trees, rocks and plants.
The most gorgeous creatures I'd ever seen

From elephants to ants!
We danced and sang all night long.
Knitted elephants can sing!

Then some time past midnight
Tucked under a butterfly's wing
I let the day come to an end
because thanks to my new wisdom
I knew each day could be spent this way
exploring grandma's knitted kingdom.

Grandma's Knitted Kingdom

Written by Rachel McRoy

Illustrated by Raquel Brandåo